Yancy & Bear

Hazel Hutchins • Ruth Ohi

Annick Press Ltd.
Toronto • New York

Early one morning, Yancy and Bear changed places.

"Good morning, Yancy!" said Yancy's mother, coming into his room. "My you're cute and curly this morning!"

Bear smiled and lifted his arms to be picked up. Yancy smiled too, beneath his painted nose, and watched over mother's shoulder as they went down to the kitchen.

"What sparkly eyes you have this morning, Yancy!" laughed Grandfather as he lifted Bear into the high chair. "Which cereal would you like for breakfast?"

Bear pointed. Yancy had always suspected that BerryNut Flakes were Bear's favourite.

After breakfast, Mother kissed them both goodbye. Bear washed his paws and face and dressed himself. He put socks on Yancy, too.

They played train while Grandfather did chores around the house. Bear drove the engine. Yancy rode in the caboose.

"Time to go shopping," said Grandfather.

With all the smells of the great outdoors calling him, Bear had quite a lot of trouble sitting quietly in the stroller. Yancy inspected the wheels.

"There's something different about Yancy today," said Mrs. MacAvity at the grocery store. She looked at Bear long and hard.

Yancy sent special thought waves to Bear. Bear turned his hat around.

"That's what it is!" laughed Mrs. MacAvity.

On the way
home they had a
picnic in the park.
Bear ate all the honey
and climbed the tallest tree. Yancy
had never been so splendidly high up before.
Grandfather had a fit and sent for
the fire department to bring them down.

That was fun, too.

When they finally
got back to the house
Grandfather wanted Yancy to take a nap, but
Bear begged to play in the sprinkler. It was,
after all, a hot day. They both got wonderfully
wet. Bear ran around and around the yard
and was dry in no time.
Yancy took a little longer.

While Yancy was hanging there, Bear
dug a huge hole in the sandbox, climbed
over the woodshed and turned thirty-
three thousand somersaults.

When Yancy
was almost dry,
they played fire
engine up and
down the sidewalk.

Bear fell off the tricycle and hurt himself.
Yancy fell too, but he didn't feel a thing.
Bear shared the band-aids with him anyway.

They staged a treasure hunt, built a fort and painted giant pictures out on the lawn until supper time.

"Looks like it was quite a day!" said Mother when she came home from work.

"I'm not sure our young fellow is going to make it through his supper," said Grandfather.

Bear was worn out. He looked like someone who had crammed a whole year of living into just one day.

By the time Mother had read them a bed-time story, Bear had barely enough energy left...

...to change back.

"We'll do it again on your next birthday," Yancy whispered as he lovingly tucked Bear into bed.

Bear was already asleep.

So was Grandfather.

Annick Press Ltd.

Annick Press gratefully acknowledges the support of the Canada Council and the Ontario Arts Council.

Canadian Cataloguing in Publication Data

Hutchins, H.J. (Hazel J.)
 Yancy and Bear

ISBN 1-55037-503-2 (bound)   ISBN 1-55037-502-4 (pbk.)

I. Ohi, Ruth. II. Title.

PS8565.U826Y35 1996   jC813'.54   C96-930220-7
PZ7.H87Ya 1996

Distributed in Canada by:
Firefly Books Ltd.
3680 Victoria Park Avenue
Willowdale, ON
M2H 3K1

Published in the U.S.A. by Annick Press (U.S.) Ltd.
Distributed in the U.S.A. by:
Firefly Books (U.S.) Inc.
P.O. Box 1338, Ellicott Station
Buffalo, NY 14205

∞ Printed on acid-free paper.

Printed and bound in Canada by
Friesens, Altona, Manitoba.